Parent's Introduction

Whether your child is a beginning reader, a reluctant reader, or an eager reader, this book offers a fun and easy way to encourage and help your child in reading.

Developed with reading education specialists, **We Both Read** books invite you and your child to take turns reading aloud. You read the left-hand pages of the book, and your child reads the right-hand pages—which have been written at one of six early reading levels. The result is a wonderful new reading experience and faster reading development!

You may find it helpful to read the entire book aloud yourself the first time, then invite your child to participate the second time. As you read, try to make the story come alive by reading with expression. This will help to model good fluency. It will also be helpful to stop at various points to discuss what you are reading. This will help increase your child's understanding of what is being read.

In some books, a few challenging words are introduced in the parent's text with **bold** lettering. Pointing out and discussing these words can help to build your child's reading vocabulary. If your child is a beginning reader, it may be helpful to run a finger under the text as each of you reads. To help show whose turn it is, a blue dot ● comes before text for you to read, and a red star ★ comes before text for your child to read.

If your child struggles with a word, you can encourage "sounding it out," but keep in mind that not all words can be sounded out. Your child might pick up clues about a word from the picture, other words in the sentence, or any rhyming patterns. If your child struggles with a word for more than five seconds, it is usually best to simply say the word.

Most of all, remember to praise your child's efforts and keep the reading fun. After you have finished the book, ask a few questions and discuss what you have read together. Rereading this book multiple times may also be helpful for your child.

Try to keep the tips above in mind as you read together, but don't worry about doing everything right. Simply sharing the enjoyment of reading together will increase your child's reading skills and help to start your child off on a lifetime of reading enjoyment!

Cute Animals

A We Both Read® Book: Level PK–K
Guided Reading: Level A

Text Copyright © 2023 by Sindy McKay
Use of photographs provided by iStock and Dreamstime.

We Both Read® is a trademark of Treasure Bay, Inc.

Published by
Treasure Bay, Inc.
PO Box 519
Roseville, CA 95661 USA

Library of Congress Control Number: 2022942085

Printed in South Korea

ISBN: 978-1-60115-374-6

Visit us online at:

WeBothRead.com

PR-10-22

Cute Animals

By Sindy McKay

TREASURE BAY

● There are so many cute animals in the world!
Some are wild animals. Some are . . .

★ . . . pets.

- Some people have pet hamsters.

Some people have pet . . .

★ . . . fish.

● Baby animals are especially cute. A baby lamb will grow up to be a . . .

★ . . .sheep.

● This baby hedgehog is called a pup.

A baby dog is called a . . .

★ . . . puppy!

- Sometimes children are called **kids**.

  A baby goat is also called a . . .

★ . . . kid!

- This baby pig is called a piglet.

  A baby cat is called a . . .

★ …kitten.

● **Tigers** are big cats. A big mama **tiger** takes good care of her little baby . . .

★ . . . tigers.

- Ducks live where there is lots of water.

  Penguins live where there is lots of . . .

★ . . . snow.

- Stingrays live in the ocean. They seem to **smile** as they swim. Dolphins also seem to . . .

★ . . . smile.

● Most birds live in trees. Baby birds

hatch from . . .

★ . . . eggs.

● Koalas live in eucalyptus trees. After lunch, they like to take a . . .

★ . . . nap.

● Chipmunks enjoy their food. Sometimes they fill their cheeks with . . .

★ . . . nuts.

- Horses like to eat carrots. Do you know another animal that likes carrots?

★ A rabbit!

● Some cute animals are big. Some cute
animals are . . .

★ ...small.

● This baby deer has spots. This baby zebra has . . .

★ . . . stripes.

● Some bear cubs are brown. Some bear
cubs are . . .

★ . . . white.

- This chimpanzee has eyes that are brown.

  Some cats have eyes that are . . .

★ . . . blue.

● This owl has big eyes. A Fennec fox
has big . . .

★ . . . ears.

A baby giraffe has a neck that is long. A baby leaf monkey has a neck that is . . .

★ ...short.

- This baby alpaca looks like it is very curious.

  So does this cute baby . . .

★ . . . COW.

41

● Which animal do you think is the **cutest**?

Maybe you think they are all . . .

★ . . . cute!

If you liked **Cute Animals**, here are some other
We Both Read® books you are sure to enjoy!

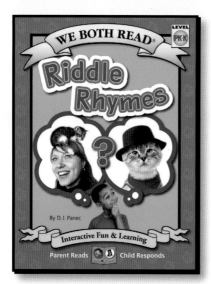

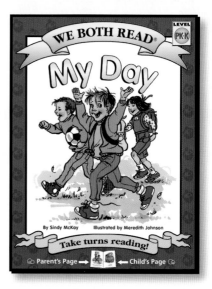

To see all the We Both Read books that are available,
just go online to **WeBothRead.com**.